# My Wor

**Black Pear Press**

# My World

First published in 2020 by Black Pear Press
www.blackpear.net

The poetry and prose included in this anthology were selected
by the judges
Sarah James/Leavesley www.sarah-james.co.uk
Tyler Keevil www.tylerkeevil.com

Cover design: Olivia Howarth

ISBN 978-1-913418-23-6

Published in Great Britain by Black Pear Press, Worcestershire

# Contents

# Introduction

This year has been a strange one for us all. We launched the Gloucestershire Writers' Network 2020 competition just as lockdown was beginning. None of us knew what the next few months would bring and how writers in Gloucestershire and South Gloucestershire would respond. The focus of this year's *The Times and The Sunday Times Cheltenham Literature Festival* is its international connections and the work they have done over the years to make the Festival more outward-looking. We decided to make our theme 'My World' and were delighted to receive the imaginative and wide-ranging responses we have come to expect.

We are very grateful to our judges Tyler Keevil and Sarah James/Leavesley for taking on the difficult task of choosing the winning prose pieces and poems. We had entries from writers all over the county, including those who live further afield but study in Gloucestershire.

Our congratulations to the winners, runners up and highly commended writers, and thanks to all who entered the competition. This year we are able to include the highly commended prose pieces and poems in our new-look anthology, published by Black Pear Press.

We look forward to seeing you again in 2021.

# Judges' Remarks

## Poetry Judge: Sarah James/Leavesley

I was delighted to spend July immersed in many different worlds, all from the comfort of my own home, as I read and re-read the poems entered for this year's competition. I was impressed by the imagination, research, crafting of words and sounds in the wide-ranging entries that included moving personal interior worlds as well as poems with historical, environmental, political and psychological elements. And yes, Covid-19 made some significant appearances too. Most poems were free verse, including some that use shape on the page, but there was also some formal verse.

Judging a competition, like any reading of a poem, is always subjective and contextual. My approach is somewhat like my process for writing—a slow whittling away: reading and re-reading the entries alongside each other, reluctantly letting go of more poems each time, my reluctance growing stronger the closer I get to my final selection.

For me, the weight of a poem overall depends not just on the weight of all the individual elements within it (imagery, sound, rhyme, form, narrative, repetition, word play, emotional engagement…) but how they all balance together in a particular poem. There's no set formula or recipe for this, more an intuitive process that differs from poem to poem.

The poems that eventually made it through to my final selection gave me not just a world but also a journey through that world, in some cases literally, in others more metaphorically. These journeys fall roughly into two types— some have very crafted, clearly hewed paths between each scene from the poem's world. Others roam more wildly or adventurously, leaving the reader space to head off the beaten-track and play their part in how to approach the world and poem's 'landmarks'.

I enjoyed and admired the crafted elegance and the dangling hooks where a small element of mystery or not-yet-quite-fully-understood pulled me back into re-reading and discovering something new every time. Comparing and weighting very different styles, approaches and content is not an easy job, but this is what I was tasked to do. I hope that my final decisions reflect the wonderful variety of the poems entered.

**Sarah James/Leavesley** is a prize-winning poet, fiction writer, journalist and photographer. Author of seven poetry titles, two novellas, an Arts Council England funded multimedia hypertext poetry narrative and a touring poetry-play, she has had poetry featured in *The Guardian, Financial Times,* Bloodaxe anthologies and *The Forward Book of Poetry 2016.* In addition to competition wins with individual poems, she was Overton Poetry Prize winner 2015 and 2020, and highly commended in the Forward Prizes with her collection *The Magnetic Diaries* (Knives Forks and Spoons Press, 2015). Other recent titles include *How to Grow Matches* (Against the Grain Press, 2018) and *plenty-fish* (Nine Arches Press, 2015), both shortlisted in the International Rubery Book Award. Her website is at www.sarah-james.co.uk. She also runs V. Press poetry and flash fiction imprint.

# Prose Judge: Tyler Keevil

Judging a literary competition is a humbling experience. There are so many talented writers out there, so many individuals with distinct voices, unique experiences, passionate views, and vital things to say. Each year, I find myself cast in a comparable role, and acting as a 'judge' of sorts, when considering the work of my Creative Writing students during the marking period. One of my own writing teachers, Matthew Francis, once told me he is continually impressed by the skill, inventiveness, and sheer creativity of his students—and I fully agree.

This is all the more the case in judging a literary competition, in which some of the entrants might be current students or alumni of similar writing programmes, or developing, established, or professional writers. To read through these entries was to go on a literary journey, perhaps in some Wellsian contraption: constant transitions through space and place and time, a myriad of voices, characters rising up and passing by, with others arriving to take their place. It was an exhilarating voyage. On display were all the best aspects of what a short story can do: they can trouble and unnerve us; they can offer snapshots of experience; they can take us out of our own life, enabling us to understand the thoughts, feelings, and lives of others; they can offer social comment and critique, and provide guidance or even comfort; they can grant insight and illumination—building to that all-elusive epiphany.

A field so strong is a mixed blessing for a judge, since it makes the reading process a delight, but the selection process difficult. Therein begins the slow, careful task of whittling the works down—beginning with a personal 'longlist' of standout work. Some excellent entries didn't quite make the top ten, simply because there could only be ten. When it comes to the stories that did, it goes without saying that they all demonstrate the qualities you would expect: control of language, originality, literary craft, grasp of story structure. Beyond that, the short length helped me make my selections. The short story is an incredibly demanding form, and the shorter the length, the harder it becomes for an author to deliver that 'literary payload'. So upon reflection, the stories I selected are those that felt the most rounded, the most resonant, the most full, the most complete. They felt as if they did not need to be any longer: they had achieved what they had set out to do, within that unyielding length requirement— and in so doing often they captured an entire life, or way of life.

If selecting the top ten was challenging, taking the next step and picking a winner, and three runners up, was even more difficult—as you can imagine. At a certain point, in reading and re-reading those entries, the process became partly intuitive. I had the printed works set down in front of me, not in a pile but laid out to give each its own space. The stories that rose to the top were the ones that had that unforgettable (and unquantifiable) quality: they stay with you, and you can't shake them. You find yourself thinking about them, even when not considering them, or sitting at your desk in 'judging' mode—and they still appear in your thoughts, even after the process is complete. I hesitate to comment on any individual author's achievements for fear of not being able to name-check them all or do them justice. These stories can and do speak for themselves. I hope you enjoy reading them as much as I did.

**Tyler Keevil** is an award-winning author from Vancouver, Canada. He writes novels, short stories, creative non-fiction, and screenplays. He has received several awards for his short fiction and filmmaking. He writes both literary and genre fiction, and his work has appeared in a wide range of magazines and anthologies including *Brace*, *Interzone*, *New*

*Welsh Review*, and *PRISM: International*.

His debut novel *Fireball* was published by Parthian Books in 2010, was longlisted for Wales Book of the Year, and received the Book of the Year People's Prize 2011. His next novel, *The Drive*, an epic road-trip adventure set in the Pacific Northwest, was published by Myriad Editions in August 2013. The book was selected as an editor's pick at Litro and Waterstones and shortlisted for the Wales Book of the Year—going on to win the People's Choice Award. In 2014, *Burrard Inlet*, Tyler's first collection of short fiction, was published. The book was nominated for numerous awards, and one of the stories from the collection, 'Sealskin,' received the $10,000 Writers' Trust of Canada/McClelland & Stewart Journey Prize. Recent publications include *No Good Brother* published by The Borough Press (HarperCollins) and in September 2020 *Your Still Beating Heart* (Myriad Editions).

He is a Lecturer in English Literature and Creative Writing at Cardiff University, and lives in South Wales with his wife and children.

www.tylerkeevil.com

## Final Gig at the Motorway Services—Marilyn Timms

A bridge, pitted by generations
of iron-clad wheels, marks
the end of the known world.
Prone upon its ancient planks,
I ease under the guard rail,
listen to the river breathe.
The world is a saccharine bubble,
centred around me alone.
The gift of a cheap tin globe,
wrapped in tissue, gaudy with ribbons,
explodes my known certainties
into never-to-be-mended fragments.
With one urge of my finger,
I spin the world on its axis.
The British Empire, unashamedly pink,
sprawls across both hemispheres,
invites an infinity of questions.
Like giant lungs, my world balloons
and shrinks with every sweet-sour answer.
Music becomes my camouflage;
honeyed armour against unpalatable truths.
Years of practice in airless rooms.
My cello is friend, lover, child.

Tonight, the noise and chatter of the room
circle around and over me, never touching.
I wheel away from the false bonhomie,
the fries and half-chewed chicken,
to the darkling sanctuary of another bridge.
Eight lanes on the midnight tarmac,

eight notes in an octave.
A single, eastern headlight mimics
a sigh from my orphaned instrument.
Plaintive at first, it grows nearer,
larger, louder; issues a summons.
A cohort of cars, a metal orchestra,
responds, spills over unseen horizons;
each headlamp a golden dragon's eye
to be pinned on my stave.
Lines of light move right, left, right;
overtaking, undertaking; twisting, turning;
weave and interleave a liquid tapestry of notes.
Rear-lights play a scarlet counterpoint
to this concerto of despair. An imagined
cello solidifies between my knees.
Insubordinate arms shuffle to attention.
Palsied fingers lift an ethereal bow,
lost in the music, knowing the score;
Multiple Sclerosis and wheelchair upstaged.

## *Winning Prose Piece*

## Strands—Robin Darrock

The strains of the song, its rhythm matching the carding of the wool, drifted in through the open door. Her fingers, slower now, still moving fluently along the loom, Cairistìona hummed along, the Gaelic as familiar to her as her own name.

She could pick out her niece's clear voice among the singers, and her great-niece's softer, pure tones. She used to sing like that, her strong young arms working the wool with the other girls, blending in with them, before taking the wool to the loom. Even as a youngster, weaving the strands had been as natural as grass growing. How had more than fifty years passed? Weaving on and on, the pattern unending.

Her niece's voice rang out in the call for tea. Cairistìona got up, flexing her gnarled fingers and wincing at the ache in her back. She rubbed it as she swung the filled kettle over the fire. Outside, the clouds lowered over the mountains behind, shrouding the tops in a mist that was working its way to the sea. It would soon be gutting time again, and the houses, echoing for weeks to the voices only of women and bairns, would welcome the men home from the fishing.

It had once been her favourite time of year—sitting by the quay in the rain and the fickle sunshine, dreaming of the possibilities. The rank smell of the herring pervaded her hair, her skin, the scales and guts slimy on her bloodstained hands, but in those days, the world opened up like an oyster. The pearl was waiting for her, when the ships came home. She would travel, she and Ruaridh, see the world, and then come home.

'Where shall we go? Down to England? Europe?'

'America, Canada, even,' Ruaridh said, elbowing her, grin quirking.

'Don't be daft.' She ruffled his red hair. 'How would we ever get to America?'

He swung her round, his brown eyes shining. 'Ah, Cairistìona, mo chridhe, the world is our oyster.'

'Oh, aye, when our ship comes in!' She was laughing in spite of herself.

Ruaridh had always said his ship would come in. Until one day, it didn't.

'Cairistìona!' Mairead burst into the front room, where she was weaving. Her dark hair was wild and windswept. 'The ship... she's gone down.'

Cairistìona didn't hesitate, merely ran out of the house. It was Mairead who picked up her shawl, thought to bring food and a light, stood by her on the quay as they waited for news.

In the end, she couldn't simply wait. The sea was calmer now, but still lashed her face with spray and half-blinded her with salt as she and cousin Domhnall and a few of the others rowed out to the wreck. For Ruaridh, it was too late.

Cairistìona sank down onto the hard seat again, hearing the singing start once more. Her fingers cracked, stiffened, and then took up the strands.

They had saved a few, though: Iain, young Daniel, Micheil Dubh... Daniel's hands had clutched her as she hauled him on the boat, and he lay in the bottom gasping like a landed fish.

When she married Daniel, life continued much as before: gutting, weaving, giving an eye to her sisters' bairns. The children she'd imagined never came, though her sisters' were almost like her own. They would take her place here, weaving the strands.

And then came the day when Daniel never came back. Once again, the sea had cheated her of her ship.

Her tea had grown cold. Cairistìona carried the cup to the sink and washed it, along with the younger women's empty mugs. Her hands, red and liver-spotted, ached. Thirty years on her own, working, scraping to put food on the table, carding, gutting, weaving.

The strands moved easily under her fingers. The singing was calming.

'Aunt Cairistìona.' Her great-niece touched her shoulder. 'I'll take over here. You rest.'

Cairistìona smiled at the young face, and shook her head. Her hands still worked, creating, and the pattern went on.

## Old Times...Christine Griffin

...when jubilant early bells summoned
shawled women to mass,
enticed old men to fierce espressos
in sloping pavement cafés

...when children shrieked through cobbled squares,
vespas whizzed past aproned market traders framed
in curtains of mortadella, salami, mozzarella

...when mornings were gossip, bursts of song,
cigarettes, grappa, warm ciabatta,
triumphant chimes from Santa Maria Maggiore

...until the solemn Angelus drew people
up worn steps, along shadowed alleys
to pungent garlic, rough bread, glistening salads,
sleepy afternoons on flowered balconies.

...later there would be music, dancing,
*pasta alla checca* on checked tablecloths,
Chianti as the sun sank.

Now bells hang lifeless in pigeoned belfries,
weeds grow round the Palazzo Vecchio,
litter washes up in empty corners.

The door to the past has slammed
on music, laughter, chatter,
will not, cannot re-open.

Silence stalks the empty squares,
friends are fearful, keep their distance.
Youths gather, hooded, mutinous,
under an indifferent sun.

13

# Earthrise—Iris Anne Lewis

An upturned bowl of porcelain,
white-marbled blue
against the blackness of the sky,
fragile and vulnerable
above the pockmarked
greyness of the moon.

Of all the planets
seen with naked human eye
Earth alone burns blue.

But its surface is alight
with colour—
red sandstone, white chalk cliffs,
the cream of limestone scarps,
the shifting hues of churning seas.

And though the Earth
is just a planetary dot
circling in the void,
it alone teems with life.

Archaea, bacteria, moss then birch.
Jungle and forests, blossom and grain.
Locusts, plankton, tigers and turtles,
nematode worms, all creeping things.

Four-stomached cows, the octopus
well-furnished with nine working brains.
Lanternfish which light up the deep,
swifts which sleep on the wing

and hairless apes who seek for knowledge,
strive to understand.

# Two Dark Shadows—Iris Anne Lewis

Look, can you see her? The child, there, playing on the beach. She is wearing blue shorts, loose t-shirt. Her hair is flying in the salt-sprayed wind.

It is morning. The tide is retreating and further out in the bay is a woman. Lissom as a seal rolling with the deep-water currents. She raises a hand and the child runs towards her. Her small feet scuff through the surf. She is up to her knees in water, then up to her hips and still her mother waves her on.

Then 'No,' shouts a deep voice. 'Come back.' A man, cheeks ruddy through sun, or perhaps anger, hurtles down the beach and into the sea, grabs the child.

I was that child. It was my sixth birthday. I remember it well—the inviting sea, my carefree mother, my father troubled.

We always felt at home on the beach, the place that shifts between land and sea. Soon after my birthday my mother taught me to swim and within days I was dipping and diving among the waves. Under my father's watchful eyes I scrambled over rocks that fringed the shore, gathered shells and pebbles. My father led the three of us on cliff-top walks, taught me to recognise the layers of sandstone and granite in the towering headland. I got to know the plants that grew on the dunes and the crags—clumps of pink thrift, sharp-spiked marram grass, the fleshy leaves of golden samphire. As I grew older the walks got longer and so my mother turned back, while my father and I went on. After a while she stopped coming on the walks, spent hours away from home, sometimes even days. When I asked, my father just said, 'She's gone to her people.' And then the time came when she didn't come back and after a while I stopped asking.

After that my father took me inland to explore—the forests and fields, the mountains and moors. I learnt to know the predatory habits of hawks; the dams and ditches built by beavers; the sloughed-off skin of snakes.

And so the days passed—on the beach, on cliffs or woodland tracks.

I'm sixteen now. It's my birthday. My father wakes me with a present. A wooden box, its surfaces teeming with hares, owls, deer, voles, bees. He has carved them all himself. 'This box is my gift to you,' he says, 'and this is from your mother.' He lifts the lid, reveals a dress packed neatly in the box.

'Wear it this afternoon,' he says. 'We'll go down to the beach, take a picnic tea.'

The meal is good, the sand warm to touch.

The sun, already dipping down to the west, bathes the bay in gold. The dress swirls in folds around my legs. It shimmers blue, green, hazy grey.

The sun is setting. 'The time has come for you to choose,' he says and turns around. I watch him walk away.


Listen, can you hear? The shush of waves on shingle, the gush and suck of water pulsing through the rocks, the cries of gulls as they glide overhead. But there is more.

From the sea, you hear a song that carries softly on the breeze. It is her mother calling.

Look! Her silken dress is soaked with surf. Her skirts cling round her legs. The waves surge in until, breast-high, they lift her off her feet and she is swimming. Still her mother's voice is singing. The rose-gold sun is sinking. She looks back to the land and sees the outline of her father climbing up the coastal path. Almost she heads back to shore but still she hears her mother calling. Her voice is low and loving. She leads her daughter further out to sea but yet once more she glances back.

16

And if you watch, you will see, silhouetted on the cliffs against the crimson sky, a figure with a hand raised in farewell. The girl swims on but first she blows a kiss to him. But all he sees are two dark shadows, swimming.

# The Wall—Tony Domaille

'Red,' said Thomas, waving his arm in a wide arc. He was five, but it was the first word he'd ever formed.

'He spoke, Mark,' said Claire and we hugged each other, but not Thomas. You can't hug Thomas.

When he was a toddler, we didn't worry too much about his not speaking. Children develop at different rates. But the silence continued. No words. No half words. Not even sounds, and we knew things weren't right. Then, when Thomas was nearly four, the paediatricians concluded he was autistic.

'Lots of kids grow up to live reasonably normal lives though, don't they, Doctor?' I asked, and Claire gripped my hand a little more tightly.

The doctor shrugged. 'Thomas's autism is profound. Communication is going to be extremely difficult for him. He may learn to say the odd word, maybe use some signs, but...'

So, we had accepted his silent world, but now he had spoken. Just one word, but where might it lead?

'Red is a lovely colour, Thomas,' I said. 'Do you like red?'

He stared at me. I knew it wasn't going to happen, but I was disappointed when he didn't answer.

Claire said, 'Do you think he wants his wall to be red?' She knelt in front of him. 'Would you like your bedroom wall to be red, Thomas?'

His face, framed in dark hair, gave no response. No change in expression.

'Can you say red again, Thomas?' I asked, but he didn't. He simply waved his little arm in an arc again towards the wall.

I called in sick the next day and I went to the DIY store. I bought red paint and painted Thomas' bedroom wall. Then I sat there, staring at the bright colour until Claire brought him home from school.

Claire held Thomas's hand as they walked into his impossibly tidy bedroom. Never a toy out of place from the neat lines he created. He showed no surprise, no excitement, no emotion. But he looked directly at the red wall and opened his mouth. We watched, transfixed, as he tried to form what he wanted to say. It sounded like he was taking short, noisy breaths, and then suddenly the word came.

He said, 'Orange,' his arm tracing that arc again towards the newly painted wall.

I don't know what I'd expected. I knew there would be no whooping with excitement, no gabbled words of wonder, or hugs of thanks. But in a moment, all my hopes that this would be a springboard to something bigger crashed.

'He doesn't like it,' I said.

Claire shook her head. 'It doesn't matter, Mark. He said another word. He said orange.'

'Do I change the colour?' I asked.

'I don't know,' said Claire.

Thomas waved his arm again and said, 'Red. Orange.'

It was pointless, but we asked him. Did he want the wall to be both colours? One colour or the other? I told Thomas I would repaint the wall if he wanted me to. I knew he understood what I was saying, but he could give me nothing.

The next morning, I slept in, so when Claire called out, 'Mark, Mark, come quickly,' I thought something was wrong.

I rushed into Thomas's bedroom, then stopped in my tracks. Thomas and Claire were sitting on the carpet. There was no crisis to be seen.

'What's wrong?' I asked

'Nothing,' said Claire. 'Thomas spoke again.'

Thomas looked at Claire and then at me. He waved his arm in that arc again and said, 'Red. Orange. Yellow.'

Claire wiped a tear from smiling blue eyes. You know what he's saying, don't you?'

I nodded. 'Richard of York gave battle in vain. He wants a rainbow on his wall. Is that what you want, Thomas?'

Our son didn't answer, but he didn't need to.

I made my second trip to the DIY store. Then I painted a rainbow on Thomas' wall. When Claire and Thomas saw my handiwork, I swear the tiniest smile started to form on our boy's beautiful, but expressionless, face. But then it was gone.

'Do you like it, Thomas?' I asked.

Thomas took his eyes off the wall and looked at both of us in turn. Then he waved his arm in an arc and said, 'Rainbow.'

I so wanted to hug him then, but that's not how it goes with Thomas. Instead, he tilted his head into his mother's arm, and I knew that was good enough.

# Uncharted—Derek Healy

Struggling to unpick a knot of roads, lanes and paths,
how easy it is to lose the way as given to me,
to end up where I was never meant to be,
a well-intentioned trespasser
on the wrong side of an argument,
showered with stones instead of flowers,
welcome as the bailiff with his list.

How easy it must be if you never go astray,
don't misread your maps,
hold fast to the rightful path;
no fear of dogs' teeth tearing at your thighs,
gashed skin as you vault over barbs,
an ankle turned on slurried stones

...but then you fail to stumble,
out of breath and bloodied,
upon a place you were never looking for,
lost in the encroaching woods;
ivy winding round its shuttered windows,
high across its crow-call echoing walls;
to one side a peeling door ajar,
daring you into darkness,
a silence of held breath
where maps won't find the way.

# Cage in the Sky—Joanna Campbell

Babies should be aired, they say, when November is stodgy with soot. A cage five floors up where the air's thin and clear is dead sensible.

Don's fixing it onto the window now. I'm staring at my cold tea while Cora fidgets in my arms. The bread isn't toasted. I'm too tired to light the grill and it's chockful of grease. Don't want to start a fire, do I?

Don opens the window and attaches the cage so it hangs outside in the sky. Squares of blue fill the mesh and the wind sends the idle dust spinning.

'Right,' Don says, leaving for work with the dry heel from the loaf. 'That'll keep her lungs filled with oxygen. It'll give you more housework time.'

His boots thump in the concrete stairwell. His whistle catches in the wind. His goodbye echoes grow fainter and fainter.

The cage hinges are squeaking. A bird flies close, its wing brushing the mesh sides which stop the baby dropping five flights to the pavement. So they say.

There's indoor netting that stops her falling back into the room. It shivers against the wall.

The nappy pail is full, a stew of shite. Blood trickles from the larder shelf. Forgot to cook yesterday's meat, didn't I. Don had to go to the corner again and get us fish and chips. Cora's milk always smells of rock salmon.

New mothers lose pieces of brain, they say. It's more than tiredness. Something else. No one knows.

'More fresh air,' Doctor said. 'For you both.'

I used to walk a mile to the café.

'Your tea's nectar,' all the thirsty men in overalls said. And all the tired women with string bags on their laps. People used to be grateful for me. You don't know you're happy, do you. You only know when you're not. I miss not knowing.

Four screws hold the two brackets to the brickwork. They're quite small, the brackets. And they whine in the wind.

I bundle Cora into the cage and secure the netting. The wind batters the mesh and it shudders. The brackets squeal as if they're straining.

Don's left a barley-sugar in my apron pocket. It's a kind thought. Or maybe he's trying to sweeten me up, make me more cheerful. Sugar pains my teeth though. God, it hurts. Babies rob the enamel, they say. They take so much away.

Cora doesn't like her cage. She turns round and gazes at me as if I've put her in prison, poor soul. I walk over to her cot in the corner of the room. The sun makes shadows of the bars on the floor and we stare at them, Cora and me.

You'd think she'd be grateful for the fresh air and the blue sky emptying itself into her lungs. Do you know, I could climb into her cot myself, get my head down for a few hours and be glad of it. If Don came home and caught me, he'd say I was off my rocker.

I can't cope with Cora's face anymore, chiding me for shoving her aside.

'It's for your good,' I keep saying, but she starts wailing.

I bundle her out of the cage, take off her bonnet and lay her down in the cot. She's still not grateful. She screams like she always does, as if life's one long torment.

I go over to the window and crawl into the cage. It's a tight fit, but I curl up small. No need for the netting. I won't let myself fall back inside.

Doctor was right. Fresh air's what I need. The hinges creak with my weight and the brackets yelp in the face of the wind. There's a grating noise, like something's working loose. And it's a happy sound really.

## Bird Feeding—Michael Newman

Mornings, mid-week,
It is never light enough before work.
I scramble breakfast, pull back curtains
To darkness, and clockwatch.

This rush to earn a crust
Denies the birds theirs.
The banks and bends of Tumbletwist Lane
Give way to trunk road's headlight procession.

Deaths on the road.
Not just birds, but badgers, too.
Returning at dusk,
After the computerised accumulation
Of office monotony,
I am again denied birdsong.

But Friday, my day off,
My prize for long service,
Offers just compensation.
From my writing desk, I watch
Both lawn and garage roof.

This Friday there has been snow,
A week too early for Christmas.
My breadcrumbs and leftovers scattered,
I could almost choreograph the next scene.

Blackbirds first,
With one dominant bully;

Then a timid thrush;
Then pied wagtails treading eggshells.
And starlings, always starlings, squabbling.

The solitary rook is a surprise.
Nervous, he half-settles;
Sees me at the window, and flies off.

December, a month for funerals.
There has been another,
And the sharp needles still puncture wounds.
Yes, tending the afflicted never fully
Prepares us for empty spaces.

These birds are my renewal,
The breadcrumbs and water
Sacramental offering.

Today, the hurt has gone.

# Developing—Catherine Brennan

'Is it true then, about the beach?'

The boy looked up at him with that solemn expression he always wore.

'Yes.'

He must have known already. It was all anyone was talking about in the village.

They walked on in silence. The boy had put on his best trainers, he noticed, the ones they'd bought together on his last visit. The sand would scuff them up. He hoped there wouldn't be trouble.

'Will it be gone completely?' the boy said at last.

He shook his head.

'I wouldn't have thought so. It'll just be...'

He left the sentence hanging. He didn't really know what would happen. He couldn't imagine. Someone in the pub had said it would slowly wear away because of the change to the tides, that the sand would all be dumped further down the coast. So someone else would end up with their beach.

'Mum says it'll be good for the village.'

It was hard not to agree. Beaches don't employ anyone, after all.

'She's probably right,' he said.

The boy looked unconvinced. He paused to kick off his trainers and wriggle his toes in the wet sand.

'Shall we play?'

The man had almost forgotten the ball under his arm. It was as much a part of the scenery as the sea and the sand. He threw it ahead and the boy ran to retrieve it like a puppy. He shouted something back, but it was lost on the wind.

It was too cold for day-trippers, so they had the place to themselves. They ranged wide across the expanse of sand, passing back and forth and falling into mutual recrimination every time the ball ended up in the sea. The boy was fun now, easy going and eager to please. The slog of bringing him down here when he was a toddler seemed an age away. And when they all used to come together, well that was another life.

The ball sailed high above his head. The boy yelled in triumph.

'It was over!' said the man.

'Yeah, over the line!'

The new trainers made fine goalposts, but the lack of a crossbar could prove controversial.

'It was top bins!' shouted the boy in consternation.

The man laughed. They agreed to disagree. The boy always had his own scoring system when they played anyway, so it was pointless to argue.

'Can we climb the rocks?'

They always did this too, though it alarmed him a lot more than the football. Children need a bit of danger, he tried to tell himself. Life was too dull and sanitised these days. But sometimes jagged rocks and pools of water seemed just a little too adventurous.

'Be careful!' he called ahead as the boy sprang about like a mountain goat.

He reached the top and sat down heavily. The boy knelt beside him.

'Is that where it's going to be?'

He pointed across the bay. Even at a distance the earth-moving equipment was visible, carving a brown scar into the land and creeping ever closer to the water's edge.

'Yes,' the man answered.

The development was coming on apace. He watched the vehicles moving back and forth like worker ants, shaping the ground beneath them and bending it to one man's will. The boy's gaze was fixed in the same direction.

'I don't see what's so great about playing golf,' he said.

It was the first time he had sounded a negative note about what was happening. The man stole a sidelong glance at the stern little face. All the upbeat marketing and propaganda hadn't fooled him then. Perhaps children were less susceptible to such things. They didn't need jobs, after all.

'It's pleasant enough. And people pay to do it.'

'People are stupid,' said the boy.

He couldn't disagree. People were stupid. And he was no exception.

'Playing on the beach is nice too,' the boy continued, warming to his subject now. 'And swimming in the sea. And they don't cost any money. Why do they have to ruin everything?'

They lapsed into silence. The man thought of his application form, sitting over there on the resort manager's desk. Why indeed?

It had grown colder while they sat there. It was time to leave.

The boy scrambled down the rocks and jumped back on to the golden sand.

'It's my beach, Dad. My world.' he said emphatically. 'I don't want it to change.'

The man put his arm around him and turned towards the road.

'I know.'

# How to Forecast During a Pandemic—Kathryn Alderman

*We cannot say precisely which butterfly, if any, may have created a given storm—Peter Dizikes.*

As if a beat of a butterfly's wings
   had voiced the wind to storm;
      raged so hard we forgot
         who we were, how once
            seasons dressed earth
            according to the weather.

One more beat and I'm spun
   outside in, trying to forecast
   through locked windows,
   but elements tumble-flip
   like conjoined snakes
   fighting their own tails.

∞

I'll weave a crown of rosemary
   and wild garlic, tidy myself
      in and out of drawers
   and scour my hostile surfaces,
scrub to the raw sheen of sorry.

When we step back to life again
   I'll hug you forever; wonder
   how one Planck length
   could fan us into chaos,
   who left us gasping in the rain.

*Note: A Planck length is the smallest unit of time.*
*The Infinity symbol ∞ is similar to a Cartesian Graph of Chaos or 'Butterfly' Theory.*

29

# Turquoise—Kim Botly

Dr Adrian Miller stepped out of the cubicle, clothes held over his arm to cover his tummy. Once his belongings were stashed in a locker he made his way awkwardly towards the swimming pool.

Pull buoys, kickboards, and fins in a jumble in a padlocked cage at the foot of the spectators' stands. The smell of chlorine, the bumps of the tiles under bare feet, the air dense with distorted splashes and shouts; he knew this world. It had once been his.

He watched the weaker swimmers, heads out of the water, wobbling jerkily forwards in an attempt to defy the laws of fluid dynamics, and told himself no one would notice if his body failed him. All they would see was another overweight, middle-aged man floundering in the water. They wouldn't notice the younger Ade trapped within.

His new swim-hat snagged painfully on his hair as he pulled it on, reminding him that he used to talc the inside of his club hat. He crouched down at the edge and sloshed the goggles around in the water before pressing them to his eyes and pulling the straps over his head, the familiar actions comforting. He lowered himself into the cold water and felt his testicles attempt to retreat into the warm sanctuary of his abdomen. Cremasteric reflex, he thought automatically.

He took a breath, let himself drop in the water and entrusted his bulgy body to muscle memory. His legs tucked in and kicked off the wall, and now he was swooshing along underwater, arms stretched out with overlapping hands. He gave two woefully underpowered dolphin kicks, his arms bent and pushed down lifting his chest clear of the water, then his legs gave a snap kick, plunging his head under as he straightened his arms again. Lift, snap, dive. Lift, snap, dive. Hiatus at the top, thump against the water with dorsiflexed feet, bubbles of exhaled breath around his face.

Ade reached the end of the length, landing triumphant hands on the wall as per racing rules.

He hung from the side and studied the impossible angle in his forearm where it met the water, its underwater twin in a world desynchronously joined to this one. Front crawl had been his best stroke, but he had been strong then. He remembered shirts that fitted his shoulders ballooning around his middle. These days the most his arms did was help a particularly hefty patient down from the examination couch, and his stomach was now the sartorial challenge. Crawl involved a complicated combination of alternating arm movements and head-turning. And he couldn't remember what to do with his legs. Kick, but how often?

He sank his arm further into the water producing the illusion of a fracture dislocation of the elbow. He was overthinking; automated movements were shy, disappearing when analysed.

He pushed off on his left side, face down to the black line and wobbling. Poor core strength, he'd have to start doing planks. He managed the switch but turned onto his right too slowly. He had only done half a stroke and was already desperate for the snatched breath which was soon exhausted. Difficult to credit he had breathed every fourth or fifth stroke in races.

By the end of the length Ade was panting but he set off again immediately. This time he imagined he was a predator locked onto its target, body swinging from side to side, arms pulling and pushing him through the water towards his prey, legs kicking slower, stronger. Remembered images merged with the present: trailing fingers rippling the water, turquoise tie-dye of light oscillating on the floor of the pool. Without conscious thought, he tumble-turned at the end of the next length, his mind cocooned by the auditory deprivation of the underwater world. There was only this breath, this movement, this body—his body—moving through this water. Nothing existed outside this exact moment, all else either yet to come or already ended.

Twenty lengths completed, and smug with his small achievement of five hundred metres—barely a warm-up set at his old club—Ade climbed out of the pool and strode to his locker.

In the men's showers he lathered his bulgy tummy with almost-fondness.

He was a swimmer again.

# Wanderings—Grace Spencer

*(A response to lines 45-51 of the Old English elegiac poem 'The Wanderer'— how much has changed?)*

watch the coot-packs      mawing in silt,
preening in gluts;      silence's queens
newly-minted.

or spot the gulls      reigning still now—
but lowering      their spearing cries
for detritus.

my mouth seems heavy in the blankness
between your names—sāre æfter swǽsne[1].
hardly headline      innovation;
but faintly new.
skylight rain falls      as muslin does
round backstage wings.

baþian brimfuglas[2]      brǽdan feþra[3],
as we discern      that ours are wax.

I, standing here,      in the roar of
all these tree-lives,      am smaller now
than ever before.

---

[1] sorrowing for the beloved
[2] sea birds bathe
[3] preening their feathers

33

# Out of Sight out of Mind—Lesley Evans

'Hello,' he says amiably, looking up from *Treasure Island* which he is reading for the umpteenth time. 'Nice to see you.'

I only went to the kitchen to make tea. I place his mug on the table next to him.

'Thank you.' he says. 'I really like this mug. You always have such nice mugs.'

It is his mug, his house. He holds up the book, showing me the picture on the worn cover of Long John Silver brandishing a cutlass.

'This is a great story,' he says enthusiastically. 'Have you read it?' He is trying to place me. He knows I am not one of his carers, but I could be his aunt, his sister or either of his daughters. He calls me by all our names interchangeably, not understanding that I'm the only one left now.

'It's a great book, Dad.' I say, giving him the clue he needs. 'You used to read it to Lizzie and me in the flat in Port Glasgow.'

'And didn't you get it into your head that you wanted a parrot, Janey?' he asks, and I smile because it is true and because, fleetingly, he knows who I am. He sips his tea.

'This is a nice mug,' he says, then pauses, concentrating, and I know that he is mustering a memory. 'In the holiday house in Dunoon, there were blue mugs with flat handles. Tam broke one once, knocked it off the kitchen table. He thought Mrs Mackay would be furious, but she was sweet about it. Such a nice woman, wasn't she?'

All of this happened when he was a child. I know that Mrs Mackay was not a nice woman, and nor was her daughter, but I don't contradict him. I change the subject, hoping that today Dad will not make the connection between Mrs Mackay's daughter and the wife who left him, left all of us, for a publican in Helensburgh, when I was barely two.

'There's a shrub by the back door that's blocking the passageway. Will you give me a hand to cut it back later?' I ask.

'Of course, sweetheart, just as soon as we've finished our tea.' He looks out of the window for a while then gets up quickly from the chair, a long lean man, still with an easy grace to his movements. 'Right,' he says purposefully. 'I'll just go and get...' he trails off uncertainly.

'Your gardening gloves,' I say gently.

'That's it.'

The gloves are in the kitchen drawer, but I hear him heading upstairs. Somewhere between the living room and the hall he will have lost all thought of them and of me. I wonder what it would be like to do the same; if, when he was out of sight, I could put him and all the associated worry and sadness out of my mind. I hold my head. It aches perpetually with the effort of patience, of trying to follow the fractured thoughts of this dear disintegrating man. Yesterday, I confirmed the arrangements for a care home. Tomorrow we will begin a regime of day visits to acclimatise him. I start to cry, overcome with remorse and with pity, as much for myself as for him.

Dad comes back quietly and finds me bent forward, rocking my grief. I try to stop, worried that my tears will alarm him, but he kneels and pulls me close against his chest. I smell his Imperial Leather soap, just as it always was. I don't care which daughter he thinks I am, the comfort of this man who was mother and father and the whole world to me and my sister, allows me, for a moment, to be small, to be soothed.

'There now,' he says, patting my back gently, 'it's not as bad as all that.' As my sobs stop, he puts his face close to mine, our foreheads touching, and crosses his eyes, an old trick to make his little girls smile. It works. I smile and hold his hand as we move through to the kitchen, retaining the precious connection for as long as I can.

'Let's get those gardening gloves then and tackle that blackthorn bush,' I say. His hand drops away from mine and he shakes his head, a polite stranger once more.

'Please excuse me,' he says 'I have to go home now. My daughters will be wondering where I've got to.'

# Landscape with Roads—Catherine Baker

I lived beside a Roman road, a child set
between heather and stunted oaks, wild
garlic and ancient sandals rotting pulpy in ditches.
I was driven along lanes, leafing past closed doors.
Seion, Ebenezer and Tabernacle.
I sat in Our Lady's beating my flat chest,
*mea culpa, mea culpa.*

Later, I saw trails hacked between green,
the red soil bleeding beneath machetes,
gardens and souls hanging in stupefied heat.
Tracks dragging, barely visible across
Aboriginal land, stealing the Dreamtime.

I took a bus to Ekaterinburg's burial pit,
stood beside the crooked cross surrounded
by an uprising of silver birch with snow falling.
I walked over an old bridge at Tolsta,
tramped in peat that fell, in the end, to sea.

There were others twirling between
banyan, sycamore, oak and oil palm.
Once, there was an ice road, creaking,
heron-feather blue under a Northern sun.

Now, I sleep beside a three-lane motorway.
At night cars swish by, a neap tide on the turn.

# Garden Party—Liz Carew

Kirsten has put together a bunch of flowers for Grandma. Not flowers out of our garden, but a bunch of wild flowers; that's one of the interests they share. I must admit Kirsten's got a good eye. The bouquet looks professional, beautifully matched and co-ordinated but wild and romantic at the same time.

'So, this is rosebay willow herb,' she tells me 'the country name is codlins and cream. Codlins, that's the Devon word for strawberries, so it's strawberries and cream.'

Kirsten is very methodical about her enthusiasms. Grandma gave her a hardbacked notebook and she has pressed flowers and stuck them in or drawn pictures of them. Then in her neat handwriting she has noted when and where found.

We haven't seen Grandma for almost fourteen weeks now. Well we have seen her on Face Time but as she says over and over, it's not the same. Grandma is classified as a very vulnerable person; she is eighty years old and has suffered all her life from severe asthma. The visits from her usual carers have continued and she has a good rapport with them but of course, the big worry is that it's not always the same carer. We live three hours' drive away and I took the decision early on that we wouldn't break any rules because, let's face it, if you break one rule then it's so easy just to carry on and break another and another one.

So today is the first time we can actually visit. We're bringing a picnic to have in Grandma's garden. I'm her only daughter (through choice) and Kirsten mine (not through choice) so this is a big day for our tiny family. Of course, Kirsten has two half-brothers and a huge family on her Dad's side so she's not really a 'lonely only'.

The drive down takes ages. The sun is shining as it has done through almost all of this strange time and today the roads are crowded. Are the crowds headed for the Dorset beaches, I wonder? Kirsten sits beside me, thumbing through her flower notebook.

'I can't wait to see Grandma.' She starts to hum. Kirsten has a particularly tuneless hum. I don't say anything. I am wondering what mood Grandma will be in.

An epidemiologist is saying on the radio, 'The virus is extremely infectious; just a handful of cases can lead to thousands.'

'Kirsten, you know we have to stay two metres away from Grandma.'

She sighs and the sigh works into her, 'Yes, Mum!'

We park and crunch up Grandma's short drive. There's Grandma at the window, looking elegant as usual, dressed in her usual bohemian style, dangly earrings with a patterned dress pulled in at the waist, her grey hair, longer of course, pulled back into a bun. As usual I'm in my trademark navy trousers and short jacket combo. Grandma's a flower artist and I'm an accountant; you can't get much more different than that.

I gesture to Grandma that we are coming through the garden gate and push it open. Grandma is standing on the patio surrounded by pots full of flowers. Don't ask me their names. I've drummed into them both they have got to keep two metres apart.

'Hi, Mum,' I smile, 'it's great to see you.'

'Yes', she answers, 'long time no see.' She looks very cross about this, as if it's all my fault. I feel relieved I don't have to give her a hug. Never mind the theatrical hugs, Mum is keen on giving several *bises* in greeting. Mum's emotions are like the flowers in her pots and paintings, they spill over all over the place.

'Well,' she says 'Anna's given me my orders, Kirsten. Shall we sit down? I've put the chairs metres apart.'

'It's to keep you safe, Mum,' I say. I am feeling concerned—after all Kirsten went back to school this week.

'Things haven't been easy, Anna,' she announces. 'I thought you'd come to see me sooner. I missed you so much.' She looks at Kirsten as she says this, narrowing her eyes slightly as if to emphasise the great distance from one end of the table to the other.

'We've missed you, Grandma,' says Kirsten and before I can stop her, she rushes up to Mum, her bunch of wild flowers held before her. There they are, my daughter and my mother, two peas in a pod, locked in a hug and framed by flowers.

# Harebushes Wood—Clare Finnimore

Too humid on our coast.
Due to leave in April,
but no flights to Madras,
he says,
dark skin
disappearing into green.

Oak, beech, hornbeam, lime,
ash, alder, quickthorn, pine.
Emerald, khaki, olive, jade,
roots, branches, nettles, ferns.

Scents of wild garlic draw me on.
You can follow me.

His voice on rustling leaves
interrupting Celtic spirits
hiding in the wood
too ancient to name.
Woodwhoses, cool verdigris, toadstool and moss
casting the spell.

Swop me your dream,
he says.
The sycamore beckons
with Sisters Wood and Ragged Hedge,
May's stage is set.

Then on a sudden, light and space,
sheep-mown grass,
the wider path.
Tarbarrow cricket pitch
and neat pavilion.

Its own amphitheatre
with no crowd.
He talks Tamil names and horses,
his mare and geldings
having no exercise.

Then descending further down again
the two paths cross.
Safer, he says
safer this way
and here.

Children's voices breaking in,
I hear cycles in the wood
singing, laughter and the sound of cars.
Through the needle barrier my dog and I,
stumbling almost onto road,
the quiet lane now a dual carriageway
I look around but he is gone.

# Moon Shadows—Jan Turk Petrie

Reaching the highest point on the moor, my car splutters and comes to a halt. One glance at the petrol-gauge tells me I've been running on empty; a stupid mistake—the latest in a long line of stupid mistakes. I'm nowhere—a place without a name more than a dozen miles from home.

Though I turn the ignition key over and over, the engine won't fire. There are no lights in any direction except for a string of them winking at me on the distant horizon like an I-told-you-so.

It may be the early hours but surely someone is bound to come along soon. In a separate timeframe, I'm already telling the tale of this breakdown, turning my lack of foresight into an anecdote that works out okay in the end.

I switch to sidelights knowing that eventually they will grow dim as the power drains away. I keep expecting to hear the drone of an approaching engine, rehearse my story ready to play the hapless victim again.

Ten minutes pass, then twenty. It's too cold, my clothes too flimsy to sit out the night here in the vague hope of being rescued. At least there's a moon tonight. Flicking off the lights, I wait for my vision to adjust before I get out, locking the door behind.

The silence is unnerving. A moment of indecision and then I pull my collar up and start walking, cursing heels I haven't worn in years—shoes that, like me, aren't intended for the great outdoors.

Spilled-out under the vast and overpowering array of stars, I feel myself shrink. Thin slivers of moonlight are caught in the puddles that punctuate the road ahead. My heartbeat speeds up to match my echoing footsteps. I glance behind to find my car, my only sanctuary, has all but disappeared.

From time to time I stop my clip-clopping to listen for a car but there's only the plaintive cry of an owl and, later, something I try not to imagine snuffling in the undergrowth.

Just as clouds start to edge out the moon another owl calls from a distance. Plunged into a deeper darkness, my scalp feels it first—the telltale sound of breathing; something or someone is behind me. I dare to look back and see nothing. *Don't be so soft*, my mother's voice tells me. *You always had an overactive imagination.*

My smile fades when the breathing resumes. Like grandmother's footsteps, it stops when I stop; starts again when I walk on. *Don't run*, Mum tells me. *You'll never outrun it.*

Rustling to my left; the acrid tang of trampled ferns; it's no longer following but walking alongside me, matching me step for step.

Could it be him come back? His double, that pale imposter, has been with me day and night since they asked me to do it. Like a fool, I'd followed that kindly policeman to where they'd laid him out in a cold room under harsh lights. Face of thunder and, not quite hidden beneath the sheet, I spotted the obscene purple bruise circling his throat, the noose's mark like some foolish tattoo he went ahead and got without telling me.

I won't look; won't give him the satisfaction. Better to pretend I can't hear all his blundering and tearing at the gorse.

When the moon re-emerges, I make out a shape—not a presence, more an absence of light. Oh the relief when it goes on by. In its passing, a sweet stench catches in my throat, pungent and familiar as a first love never forgotten. But it comes to a halt, blocks the way ahead—a black mass waiting for me where the road divides. My newly adjusted eyes pick out its back, a tail and two pricked ears brought forward. Listening.

With a low, encouraging grumble, the pony invites me to come closer. They call it nickering—this promise of gentleness. Remembering, I take care to approach at an angle.

No sudden movements, I must keep in its line of sight. I reach up to stroke reassurance into its withers. 'It's okay,' I tell the animal over and over. My fingers are drawn to the velvet skin of her muzzle. She snorts, her hot grass-laced breath in my face. Leaning into the warmth of her flank, I'm the girl I once was, not the townie I became. Behind the pony's back, four white fingerposts float out of the darkness. She's here to show me a way forward.

# Hidden—Val Ormrod

The silence in the air hangs
heavy as nimbus about to break.
Days jitter by.

No longer able to comfort
with the fluffy cumulus of hugging
or risking cirrus kisses,

we circle each other, wary-eyed,
terrified to touch,
or hunker down in lonely isolation.

A black cloud, swollen with menace,
fills our heads like the shadow
of a huge predatory bird.

All around, a hidden terror
reaches out, eager to scatter chaos
inside each new host,

every human a potential enemy
whose touch or exhalation
could pass us a fatal gift.

We have no idea what the ending
will be, or even if there will be
an ending

to a nightmare
that begins afresh each morning
as, head heavy as a heap of wet earth,

we listen to the daily toll of death.

We can't hide from it forever,
scientists say.

This is our world now. So we wait
with foreboding, wait for that first
unbidden cough.

# Late Fuel—Michael Hurst

There's something reassuring about the Shell garage logo. The stylised scallop shell. The easy splay of the segments. The bold colours. A design that's survived for decades. It speaks to us, that logo, of the quality of the product, of the global reach of the company. It's more important than you or me. Hell, it's more important than the country, more important than capitalism. The corporate flag is stateless. It's a privilege to be allowed to exchange our puny local currency for such a quality global product.

True, the blood-red highlighting is unfortunate. Look at the sign in a certain way and it is soaked in blood. Global blood, blood of the earth.

I notice these things. Branding. It's part of my job.

Tonight I only see a bright reassuring logo, not a bloody one. It's the middle of May. I've come out for fuel I don't need. Hardly anyone's driving in lockdown.

An empty petrol station on a dark wet evening is a lonely place. Hopperesque. The illuminated canopy keeps me dry but the rain-chill in the air is a reminder that I'm outdoors. I've parked at a pump close to the forecourt store. As I wait for the petrol I glance at the shop window and see that I'm not the only one here. A girl's on duty and she's laughing with a short bald man who's standing on the customer side of the counter. The girl takes a while to authorize my pump. She does it without looking away from the bald man.

The motors buzz and the Shell petrol starts flowing.

Baldie is entertaining the shop girl. He bobs up and down, rubbing his scalp. She has a pretty face when she's laughing.

As I enter the shop Baldie pulls a Covid mask over his mouth. Then the girl does the same.

Baldie is not a regular customer. He's holding a collection tin and there's a Help for Heroes promotional box on the counter.

I ignore him and get out my bank card as the girl processes my order.

Her nametag says Michelle. It makes me smile. Chelle at Shell. I know better than to say anything of course.

My name is Charles. A decent solid branding.

I stop smiling. It's mean-spirited. I wouldn't have cared normally, but the laughter I saw through the window between the girl and Baldie was so spontaneous, so innocent that I feel ashamed.

Baldie shakes his tin. 'Care to make a donation, sir?'

His voice is squeaky as though he's cultivated a beta-male persona to mollify the alphas.

Help for Heroes. The silhouetted logo of the soldiers carrying the stretcher is almost as recognizable as the bleeding scallop outside.

'I have charities I donate to each month,' I say.

Someone said that at work.

'It's a very good cause,' says the girl.

Baldie holds out the tin at arm's length in a concession to social distancing. I push in a pound coin.

'Thank you, sir.'

He doesn't sound very grateful.

Bloody Help for Heroes—when did charities become beauty contests? It's populism, pure and simple. Who's shaking a tin for the shouty old men with mental illnesses?

Baldie has picked up on something in my face. 'Perhaps you don't approve?' he says.

'I do, I do. The squaddies, the injuries…'

'It's just that…?' says Baldie, with a sly expression.

'It's just that whenever I see actual squaddies they always look a bit…'

'A bit what?'

'Well. A bit rapey.'

'Rapey?' he says in his squeaky voice.

The girl's eyes widen and I can tell she is unimpressed,

despite the mask.

Charlie, Charlie...Anything you could have said would have been better:

I don't donate to Help for Heroes because of the pointless alliteration.

If governments send men and women into war, *they* should pay for their help when they get home.

Even the populism thing—the unglamorous shouty old men—would have been better.

It's my world versus their world. There's nothing to do but leave.

Outside, the forecourt is still empty. A swoosh of tyres comes from the wet road. Another lockdown driver.

Through the window, Baldie and the girl are laughing again. They're not looking at me.

Baldie's car is parked on the concrete apron beside the shop. It's a crappy French model. I ease past in my Audi under the Shell sign, which shines out as brightly as ever.

## Judge: Sarah James/Leavesley

### The Rain's Tale—Sarah James

Overnight, the rain has tried
to press its story through the window
and into our eyes, ears and mouths.
It has failed, leaving instead a trace
of whatever we choose to read
in the poised beads on the glass.

Each drop is a glistening glimpse
of the world around us, reflected
as nothing more substantial
than a pause in flowing water,
with snatches of city bricks, tired grass
and patches of grey or blue—
the landscape and sky fragmented.

I fear that all caught light
eventually drips away
in trickles of condensed cloud,
heavy with missed chances.

But my worries are not the water's,
wet with the world's origins
and its endless recycling.
First breaths rose from this
and last breaths return to it.

My life's a swilled atom in this flood,
floating a while on the skylit surface,
before slowly sinking back.
Sometimes, if I listen closely
to the rain as it's falling, I hear
it softly calling out my name.

## At Night—Sarah James

The brightest star is the one I want,
though it's way beyond my grasp.

When a constellation dies in space,
its light lives on for those watching here,

millions of miles and lifetimes away.
They say that every star is a wish.

I look up at tonight's cloudless sky:
hauntingly clear of mist—alive

with dazzling wishes. Yet the only star
I want is the one that's already dead.

# Judge: Tyler Keevil

## Scalped—Tyler Keevil

Extracted from *Burrard Inlet* (Parthian)

Today is my last day on the barge, and I've been consigned to the ice bins. Roger's got me oiling the chains that pull the rakes. I'm spraying them down with an industrial-strength lubricant. What I do is this: I shake up the can, making the widget clack, and hose down a series of links. Then I wait while the lube leeches in, foaming and sputtering and creating a kind of lather, stained brown by rust and grease. Afterwards, I slot the end of my crowbar into each link and bend it back and forth, back and forth, slowly freeing up the pins. Every herring season the salt air causes the chain-links to rust, and every year we go through this ritual to loosen them and prevent them from seizing up. I've started with the starboard bin. All the ice has been cleared out—we did that a few weeks back—but in here it's still cold and damp as the bottom of a well, and the leftover moisture is oozing down the walls and pooling on the fiberglass floor. The power has to be shut off, for safety reasons, so my main light source is a halogen work lamp, strung in on an extension cord from the lower deck.

Roger and I were supposed to be doing this together, but last night he got a call from our supplier. The new alternator for the motor in one of our ice-making machines was ready, and he had to go pick it up—way the hell out in Delta. That was his reasoning, anyway. But I figure it's also partly my punishment for telling him that I'm leaving, for abandoning ship.

He seemed to take a certain satisfaction in explaining my duties to me.

'You'll be on your own in the bins, greenhorn,' he said.

'I can handle it.'

We were up in the lounge: me on the sofa and him sitting in his big reclining chair—his captain's chair. Doreen had already gone to bed. In the evenings she likes to retire early, as she calls it.

'I'll be back later on. Until then, you're in charge.'

'Captain for a day, eh?'

'That's right. Just watch yourself on them rakes.'

'I'll be careful.'

To do this work, the chains and rakes have to be at head height. The rakes are metal girders that span the whole width of the bin. Each one is studded with two-inch steel spikes, for combing and flaking the ice. I am very wary of these spikes, hovering at the edge of my vision, glinting in the half-light like the claws of a hawk. I've always had a thing about the rakes. Now that we're back in dock the nightmares have settled, but I won't fully relax until I'm safely ashore, and have put some distance between me and them. For now, for today, I move very carefully: ducking and stooping and lurching about with a hunchbacked gait.

At around two o'clock I run out of oil. We have more canisters up top, in the storage cupboard in the breezeway. Leaving my crowbar on the floor, I crab-walk sideways towards the door of the ice bin—keeping my head tilted at an angle, bending low beneath each rake. I've left the door open for the extra light it affords, and the entrance is a pale square in the dark, like the far end of a tunnel. Against it, the rows of rakes stand out in stark silhouette.

At the last rake, right near the door, I misjudge my step—or maybe the rakes lurch a bit, making a sudden movement just as I duck under. The tension in the chains causes them to do this, occasionally, and in this case it's as if they're reaching out for me. Something connects with my head and my neck crackles and then I am on the floor. I am on the floor and there is this searing, scorching pain in my scalp, right atop my skull. I clutch at the spot, twisting and squirming and arching

54

my back as if the pain is electrocuting me, coursing through my whole body. I don't cry out—there's nobody to hear me cry—but what I do is make these soft whimpering noises, almost childish. And for a moment, in my pain-addled panic, I have the crazy thought that what I've always feared is actually happening: the rakes are coming for me, lurching into life and slowly descending, to break me and mangle me before I can get off the barge for good.

I'm so convinced of this that I open my eyes to check. But the rakes aren't moving—they just hang there, glistening like obsidian. Eventually the scalding pain dulls to something more tolerable: a kind of branded feeling, like when you've burnt your hand on the stove. I sit up slowly, testing my neck. It's kinked, and I can feel the tendons creaking, but it seems okay. Then I shake off my work gloves and feel my head. The hair is wet and matted and when I inspect my fingers they are sticky-slick with red. The sight makes me think of a phrase Roger is fond of using: *bleeding like a stuck pig.* I'm bleeding like a stuck pig.

'Hell,' I say, and the word bounces around me in the darkness. 'Aw, hell.'

Eventually I pick myself up. Just outside the ice-bin doors, on the lower deck of the barge, there's a bathroom that we use while we're on shift—delivering ice or servicing boats. I stagger in there and splash cold water over my head, then scrunch-up some toilet paper and press it to my scalp, trying to staunch the bleeding. It stings like acid. I perch on the toilet and have a bit of a think, debating just how in the hell I'm gonna explain all this to Doreen.

*Burrard Inlet* (Parthian Books, 2014) is available direct from the publisher, via your local bookstore (ISBN978-1910409978) and on Amazon.

# *Writers' Biographies*

**Kathryn Alderman** lives in Upton St Leonards. She won Cannon Poets' 'Sonnet or Not' and was a GWN Competition Runner-Up (2012). She's widely published in anthologies, online and print magazines e.g. Ink, Sweat & Tears, Atrium Poetry, The Poetry Bus Magazine, Eye Flash Poetry Journal and Pocket Pamphlet. Her poetry is in Luke Jerram's 'Of Earth and Sky' exhibition. @OfEarthandSkyLJ @kmalderman1

**Catherine Baker**, from Tewkesbury, has been published by Stand, Snakeskin, Atrium and Amaryllis. She was highly commended in the Prole Poet Laureate competition 2020. She has poems in anthologies such as 'Poetry from Gloucestershire' and 'Ways to Peace'. She was runner up in GWN poetry competition 2018.

**Kim Botly** grew up in London and has lived in China and France; sometimes she can't find the right word in three languages simultaneously⬛⬛⬛⬛⬛⬛⬛ and is currently putting her thriller through its paces with the Curtis Brown Six-Month Novel-Writing Course. A former NHS doctor, she tweets @KimBotly_Writer.

**Catherine Brennan** is a local writer, based in Winchcombe. She works as a tutor at the Open University and is currently studying towards a Masters in Creative Writing.

**Joanna Campbell's** collection of prize-winning stories, 'When Planets Slip Their Tracks' (published by Ink Tears) was shortlisted for the Rubery Book Award and longlisted for The Edge Hill Prize. 'A Safer Way To Fall', her novella-in-flash, was published by AD Hoc Fiction. Her flash-fiction came second in the 2017 Bridport Prize. She lives in Bisley.

**Liz Carew** grew up near John o' Groats and is inspired by the countryside and culture of her homeland as well as that of Gloucestershire where she lives in Cirencester. She has been published in various magazines and anthologies and is a member of Catchword Writing Group.

**Robin Darrock**, from Cheltenham, has had articles, short stories and a national award-winning poem published under another name and belongs to several local writing groups. A Humanities graduate of the University of Oxford, Robin has worked in education and research. Robin enjoys travelling, walking, history and trying to cook.
Twitter @RobinDarrock, Facebook, or visit www.robindarrock.com.

**Tony Domaille** writes primarily for the stage and has had a number of award-winning plays published. His play 'Me & You' won the 2020 Avon Short Play Festival competition. He's had numerous short stories published in magazines and anthologies, as well as enjoying a number of competition successes. He lives in Thornbury.
https://www.facebook.com/pg/tonydomaillewriting/posts/?ref=page_internal

**Lesley Evans,** after half a lifetime as a lawyer and business leader, is studying creative and critical writing at the University of Gloucestershire and reinventing herself as the writer she told her childhood self she would one day become. She wonders why she waited so long! She lives in Cheltenham.

**Clare Finnimore**, from Cirencester, has only recently ventured into writing poetry. She has had success with writing radio scripts, including 'When Will it Be Me?' a comedy for Bath Fringe Festival, 'An Ordinary House' for Ragged Foils

Productions, and 'Started Early Took my Guide Dog' for Little Lost Robot.org in Bristol. clare@clarefinn.co.uk

**Christine Griffin** has been writing poetry and prose for many years and is widely published both locally and nationally including in Acumen, Snakeskin, The Dawntreader and Writing Magazine. Successful competition wins in 2020 include first prize in The Evesham Festival of Words competition and in the Graffiti Magazine poetry competition. She lives in Hucclecote.

**Derek Healy** has recently moved to Malvern but is a longstanding member of the Cirencester-based Catchword writing group. This is his fifth time being successful in the GWN competition. He has had work published in a number of journals here and in the States. His second collection 'Home' was published recently by Graffiti Books. dch.derekhealy@gmail.com

**Michael Hurst's** stories are published by The Fiction Desk, Ellipsis Zine, Gemini and Stroud Short Stories. He was shortlisted for the 2018 Newcomer Prize. His writing has also been performed by Show of Strength Theatre Company. Michael lives in Cheltenham with his wife and daughter. He lives in Cheltenham.

**Iris Anne Lewis** lives in Kempsford. She writes poetry, short stories and has made her own poetry films. Her work has been published online and in print, most recently in Artemis and Black Bough Poetry. In 2018 she founded the Cirencester Poetry Group. This is her sixth appearance at the GWN event. Twitter: @IrisAnneLewis

**Michael Newman** was born in 1943, and his first home was Little Washbourne, then and now the smallest village in England. He now lives in Bishops' Cleeve. He won the

Cheltenham Competitive Festival in 1994, 2000, 2002 and 2005. The Cotswold countryside has always influenced his writing. Poems are his public diary, to express the inexpressible.

**Val Ormrod** is an author and poet with awards in national and international competitions. Her work has featured in publications including Ink Tears, Stroud Short Stories, Graffiti, Eye Flash, and Hedgehog Poetry. She has an MA in Creative Writing and runs workshops in the Forest of Dean for both children and adults. She lives in Lydney.
https://twitter.com/Ladybear6

**Grace Spencer**, from Stroud, is currently studying English at Oxford University, where she loves being part of a poetry writing group. She was surprised by the poignancy of the Old English poetry she studied during her first year and was inspired to write her piece. grace.spencer13@yahoo.co.uk

**Marilyn Timms** is absolutely delighted to be the winner of this year's GWN poetry competition, having been runner up in both categories of the competition several times before. Marilyn's second poetry collection, 'Deciphering the Maze', written in collaboration with husband Howard, was published in 2020 by Indigo Dreams. She lives in Cheltenham.

**Jan Turk Petrie,** from Painswick, is a former English teacher and holds an MA in Creative Writing. Alongside her short stories, she's written six published novels: 'The Eldísvík Trilogy'—near future Nordic thrillers; 'Too Many Heroes' and 'Towards the Vanishing Point'—50s thrillers, and 'The Truth in Lie'—contemporary literary fiction. Author website: https://janturkpetrie.com

# Organisers' Note

The Gloucestershire Writers' Network is committed to keeping you in touch with all good things about the written word in Gloucestershire and South Gloucestershire. Our monthly newsletters and the website connect you with groups and events and help celebrate local success stories. This year we have added 'Online Resources' to our website to help writers find ways of connecting when face-to-face meetings have not been possible.

We were very sorry to say goodbye to Guy Hunter who has been a much-valued member of our team and as webmaster has made a huge contribution to developing the website. We are delighted to welcome Ross James Turner to take over the role.

The GWN is a non-profit making organisation and welcomes sponsorship or donations. Email pennygwn@gmail.com for details. We are always looking for ways to develop, and welcome feedback. To share writing information or sign up to our newsletter, please visit: www.gloswriters.org.uk

After much uncertainty for live events this year, The Times and The Sunday Times Cheltenham Literature Festival has been able to proceed in a new format including live-streamed events. We are grateful to them for once again creating the opportunity for our winning writers to showcase their work at their prestigious Festival.

**The GWN Team:**

Penny Howarth—Co-Chair
Rod Griffiths—Co-chair
Judith van Dijkhuizen—Co-Chair, Treasurer, Competition Administrator

Chris Hemingway—Newsletter
Sharon Webster—Publicity
Ross James Turner—Webmaster

*We would like to pass on our heartfelt thanks to our sponsors*

**Liggy Webb**
www.liggywebb.com

**Cheltenham Arts Council**
www.cheltenhamartscouncil.co.uk

**Helene Hewett of the Suffolk Anthology Bookshop**
www.theanthology.co.uk

*We gratefully acknowledge the support of*

**Cheltenham Festivals**
www.cheltenhamfestivals.com/literature

*Our thanks also to Olivia Howarth for maintaining the website.*

## Gloucestershire Writers' Network
www.gloswriters.org.uk

 @GWNgloswriters

 www.facebook.com/groups/GlosWriters/